≥ Campground Creature ≤

MOLLY MAC

by MARTY KELLEY

PICTURE WINDOW BOOKS
a capstone imprint

For Barbara Ballou, Sarah Chapman, and all the
great staff and friends of the Whipple Free Library—Marty

Molly Mac is published by
Picture Window Books
A Capstone Imprint
1710 Roe Crest Drive
North Mankato, MN 56003
www.mycapstone.com

Text © 2019 Marty Kelley
Illustrations © 2019 Marty Kelley

Education Consultant: Julie Lemire
Editor: Shelly Lyons
Designer: Ashlee Suker

Library of Congress Cataloging-in-Publication Data
Names: Kelley, Marty, author, illustrator.
Title: Campground Creature

ISBN 978-1-5158-2385-8 (library binding)
ISBN 978-1-5158-2389-6 (paperback)
ISBN 978-1-5158-2393-3 (eBook PDF)

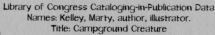

Printed in the United States of America.
PA017

★ Table of Contents ★

All About Me!

A picture of me!

Name:
__Molly Mac__

People in my family:
__Mom__
__Dad__
__Drooly baby brother Alex__

My best friend: __KAYLEY!!!!__

I really like:
__Crunchy delicious tacos!__
__But not if they have tomatoes on them.__
__Yuck! They are squirty and wet.__

When I grow up I want to be:
__An artist. And a famous animal trainer.__
__And a professional taco taster. And a teacher.__
__And a super hero. And a lunch lady. And a pirate!__

My special memory: __Kayley and I camped in my__
__yard. We made s'mores with cheese. They__
__were surprisingly un-delicious.__

Chapter 1

No Toaster, No Tacos

Krrrshhhh. Krrrshhhh.

Molly Mac slid the toaster oven across the counter toward her backpack.

"Molly Mac?" asked Mom.

"Don't ask," said Molly.

"I'm asking," said Mom. "What are you doing with the toaster oven?"

"I'm packing it for our camping trip," Molly said. "Tonight is Taco Night. I need the toaster oven to warm the taco shells."

"Well, Molly—"

"I will also need the fridge, so the cheese stays fresh!" said Molly.

Mom slid the toaster oven back where it belonged. "We're going camping, Molly," she said. "No toaster ovens. No tacos. We are going to cook dinner over a campfire tonight!"

Dad walked into the kitchen and picked up a cooler. "And we'll be toasting marshmallows!" he sang as he opened the kitchen door to go outside. "Marshmallows are my favorite vegetable. I'm going to eat about a million of them!"

Molly sighed. "I was hoping to eat about a million tacos tonight," she replied.

"Did somebody say tacos?" Grandpa Kevin asked. He walked into the kitchen holding Molly's baby brother, Alex. "Maybe Alex and I will eat tacos all weekend while you folks are off in the woods."

Alex gurgled and laughed.

Molly patted Grandpa Kevin on the
shoulder. "Sorry, buddy," she said. "Neither of
you has enough teeth to eat crunchy tacos."

Grandpa Kevin laughed. "You know what
I do have, though?" he said.

"An emergency taco kit that I can take
camping?" Molly asked.

"Even better," Grandpa Kevin told her. He
handed Molly a small, wrapped present. "This
is from Gram and me."

Molly
unwrapped the
present. It was a
shiny red camera.

"We got it so
you could take
some fun pictures of your camping trip this
weekend," Grandpa Kevin explained. "You can
show us the pictures when you get back."

"Wow!" Molly
cried. "Thanks!"
She gave Grandpa
Kevin a big hug
and held up the
camera. **"Say
cheese!"**

Click!

"That's exciting," Mom said. "Did you know that our newspaper has a photo contest every week? You could send in one of your pictures. They might put it in the paper."

"Really?" Molly asked. "I could be a real, live, professional picture-taker! Let's get going! I have some exciting pictures to take!"

"We will leave as soon as Kayley gets here," Mom said. "Are you all packed?"

Molly nodded. "Almost," she said as she picked up her backpack. "I just need one more thing. Where do we keep the hippo spray?"

"Hippo spray?" Mom asked.

"Don't ask," Molly said as she ran up to her room.

Chapter 2

Wild Hippos!

Molly and Kayley sat in the back of the car.

"This is going to be so much fun," Kayley said. "Thanks for inviting me to come camping with you."

"I'm glad you came," Molly told her. "Everything is more fun with you." She held up her camera. "Say **Tacos!**"

Kayley laughed. **"Tacos!"**

Click!

"I'm going to be a real, live, professional picture-taker," Molly said. "And my amazing picture is going to be in a real, live newspaper!"

"Wow!" Kayley said. "What are you going to take a picture of?"

Molly leaned over toward Kayley. "That's the most exciting part!" she whispered. "Since we will be out in the woods, I am going to take a picture of a wild hippo!"

Kayley's eyes grew wide. "A wild hippo?" she gasped.

Molly nodded. "There is one problem, though. I couldn't find any hippo spray. It's like bug spray. Except it keeps hippos from squishing you when you take their picture."

Kayley shook her head. "I don't think there are any hippos in the woods around here, Molly," she said.

"Are you sure?" Molly asked. "I read that they live near rivers in Africa. There is a river at the campground, and we have to drive for almost two hours to get there. After driving for that long, we'll probably be in Africa."

"I don't think so," Kayley told her.

Molly's shoulders slumped. "How can I be a professional picture-taker if there are no wild hippos to take pictures of?"

Kayley smiled and opened her bag. She pulled out her stuffed dog. **"I brought Herman!"** she said as she laughed.

Molly held up her camera. "Look wild, Herman," she said.

Click!

"I don't think Herman is wild enough," Molly sighed.

Kayley took a book out of her bag. "How about this?" she asked. She held it up so Molly could see the title—*Bear and Rabbit Go Camping.*

"A book?" Molly groaned. "A book is even less wild than Herman. A book is the exact opposite of wild."

Kayley opened the book and pointed to the picture. It showed a bear and rabbit toasting marshmallows over a campfire. The rabbit was saying, "I love toasted marshmallows." The bear was saying, "Me, too!"

"Rabbits like toasted marshmallows," Kayley said to Molly. "It says so right here in the book. We have marshmallows. Maybe a rabbit will come to our campsite. Then you can take its picture!"

Molly looked at the picture. "The book says that bears like toasted marshmallows, too! Bears are **WAY** more exciting than rabbits. I'm going to take a picture of a bear!"

Kayley shook her head. "That's not a good idea, Molly."

"I know," Molly said. "It's a **GREAT** idea."

Bigfoot

Crack! Snap! Crrrrrack!

At the campground, Dad made a roaring fire in the fire pit. Mom helped Molly and Kayley put hot dogs on sticks so they could cook them over the fire.

"Are you sure we can't toast tacos over the campfire?" Molly asked.

"Positive," Mom said. "We can have tacos anytime."

"Like right now?" Molly asked.

Mom sighed. "No, Molly. **No tacos.** Cook your hot dog."

Kayley held up her stick. "Mine has two points!" she said. "I can cook two hot dogs at once!"

Dad held up a stick with lots of small branches on the end. "Well, I can cook a million hot dogs at once!" he said as he

laughed. "And then, when we're ready to toast marshmallows, I can cook a million of them, too!"

"Speaking of marshmallows," Molly said, "could I possibly have a few marshmallows for later?"

"I'm pretty sure that there won't be any marshmallows left after Dad starts eating them," Mom said. "He's totally **koo-koo** about marshmallows. And do I even want to know why you want marshmallows for later?"

"Probably not," Molly said. "I want to take an exciting picture, but there are no hippos in the area. Herman isn't wild enough, but Kayley's book says that rabbits love toasted marshmallows. But they're not as exciting as bears who also love marshmallows."

"Bears?" Mom said.

"Bears?" Dad said.

"Bears," Molly said. "They really **LOVE** marshmallows. It was in a book, so it must be true. I'm going to stick some marshmallows in my sleeping bag. When a bear comes to eat them, I can take its picture."

"Molly—" said Mom.

"I'll have an exciting picture so I can be a professional picture-taker," Molly said. "Then I'll feed marshmallows to the bear so it won't eat me."

"Molly, honey," Dad said. "There are no bears around here. And even if there were, you shouldn't feed animals. Marshmallows are not good for them." He popped a marshmallow in his mouth. "But they're great for me. And do you know who else likes marshmallows?"

PLEASE DO NOT FEED THE ANIMALS. (NOT EVEN MARSHMALLOWS)

"Who?" Molly asked.

Dad slid a bit closer to the fire. "Bigfoot," he whispered.

"Bigfoot?" gasped Molly and Kayley.

Dad nodded. "Bigfoot. He's a big, hairy creature who lives in the woods."

"A big, hairy creature?" cried Molly. "Like Uncle Dave?"

"Not like Uncle Dave," Dad said. "Bigfoot is even bigger and hairier than Uncle Dave."

"Whoa!" Molly gasped. "I didn't think that was possible."

Dad pointed to the dark woods around the campsite. Orange light from the fire danced in the tree branches. "Nobody knows what he really is or what he looks like," he said.

"Why not?" Molly asked. "Can't they just look him up on the Internet?"

"They could," Dad said, "but nobody has ever taken a good picture of him. Some people say he's not real. But other people think he could be anywhere.
Even right here!
GRRRRRR!" Dad growled and held his flashlight under his chin.
"GRRRRRRRR! GIVE ME YOUR MARSHMALLOWS!!"

Molly and Kayley both screamed.

"All right," Mom said. "I think that's enough scary campfire stories. Who wants some marshmallows?"

After eating lots of gooey, toasted marshmallows, Molly and Kayley climbed into their sleeping bags.

"I'm glad there are no bears around here," Kayley said. "But now what are you going to take a picture of?"

Molly smiled and held up her camera. "Oh, I'm going to get a picture of something way better than a bear."

"Herman?" laughed Kayley. She held Herman up to the camera.

Click!

"Even better than Herman," Molly said. "I'm going to get a picture of **Bigfoot**."

Chapter 4

Littlefoot

Ziiiiiiiiiiiiip.

The next morning, Molly slipped out of her sleeping bag. She grabbed her camera and opened the tent. She poked her head out.

"Wow!" she said.

She shook Kayley awake. "Kayley! Kayley! You have to see this! Wake up! Wake up!"

Kayley rubbed her eyes and yawned. "What is it?" she asked.

Molly pointed to the tent flap. **"Come see! Come see!"**

Kayley groaned and rolled over.

Molly shook her shoulder. "Come on!"

Kayley wiggled out of her sleeping bag and crawled over to the opening. She poked her head out. "What?" she asked. "I don't see anything."

Molly slipped past Kayley and hopped out of the tent. She pointed to the ground. **"Look!"** she cried. **"Bigfoot was here!"**

"Bigfoot?" Kayley asked. She climbed out of the tent and looked where Molly was pointing. There were a lot of small footprints in the soft ground.

"Those feet don't look very big to me," Kayley said.

Molly pointed to the picnic table. "And look what Bigfoot did!"

The bag of marshmallows was torn apart. Small pieces of it were scattered on the table.

Molly took a picture of the shredded plastic.

Click!

She took a picture of the footprints on the ground.

Click!

"I can't believe I didn't get a picture of Bigfoot," Molly groaned. "How did we sleep through a Bigfoot attack? He must have been here for hours. He ate ALL the marshmallows!"

Kayley shook her head. "These footprints are really small, Molly," she said. "I don't think this was Bigfoot."

Ziiiiiiiiip!

Mom unzipped her tent flap and climbed out of the tent.

"Good morning, girls," she said. "What are you doing up so early?"

"Ahhh!" Molly cried. **"It's not Bigfoot. It's Bedhead!"**

She took Mom's picture.

Click!

"Very funny," Mom grumbled. "What are you doing out here?"

Molly pointed to the ground. "Bigfoot was here!" She pointed to the mess on the picnic table. "He ate the rest of our marshmallows!"

Mom looked at the footprints on the ground. "Molly," she said. "Those are not Bigfoot tracks. There is no such thing as Bigfoot. Dad was just telling you a spooky campfire story last night."

"No such thing as Bigfoot? Then what made these footprints?" Molly asked. "And what ate our marshmallows? Do you think it was a hippo? I **KNEW** I should have brought hippo spray!"

Mom shrugged. "They look like raccoon footprints," she said. "Dad must have forgotten to pack away the marshmallows before we went to bed. I'm going to get a sweatshirt. Then we can clean up and have some breakfast."

Mom climbed back into her tent.

"I'm glad it wasn't Bigfoot," Kayley said. "He sounded kind of scary. Now maybe you can take a picture of a raccoon!"

"It wasn't Bigfoot," Molly said. "And it wasn't a hippo. And I don't think this was a raccoon, either."

"Then what do you think made these footprints?" Kayley asked. "Your mom said it was a raccoon."

"I think Mom just said that so we wouldn't be scared," Molly said. She held up her camera.

"Maybe," said Kayley.

"But I'm not scared," Molly continued. "I'm excited. I didn't get a picture of Bigfoot, but now I'm going to get a picture of something even more exciting. I'm going to get a picture of . . . **Littlefoot!**"

Chapter 5

Bathroom Bigfoot

After breakfast, Molly and Kayley walked along the road through the campground.

Kayley pointed at a small butterfly on a flower. "You could take a picture of a butterfly!"

Molly sighed. "A butterfly isn't an exciting, wild animal. We need to find **Littlefoot.** We don't have much time. Mom and Dad said we could walk around this loop while they drink coffee."

"Then we're going swimming in the river!" Kayley said. "I can't wait!"

"I'm still hoping that we might see a hippo at the river," Molly said.

"I don't think so, Molly," Kayley said. She pointed to a branch in a tree. "There is a bird over in that tree. You could take a picture of a bird."

Molly sighed again. "This campground has some pretty disappointing wild animals," said Molly. "We really need to find **Littlefoot.**"

Molly kicked a pinecone. It tumbled along the road and settled in some leaves. She ran over to it to kick it again. **"Look!"** she cried.

Kayley ran over to look.

Molly pointed at the ground. "More of Littlefoot's tracks!" she whispered. "Let's follow them! Maybe they will lead us to his top-secret underground lair."

Molly trotted along the side of the road, following the trail of small footprints. Kayley crept along beside her. "What are we going to do if we find Littlefoot's top-secret underground lair?" Kayley asked.

"We will sneak in and take his picture!" Molly said.

"I don't think this is a good idea, Molly," Kayley said. "What if Littlefoot **EATS** us?"

"He's not going to eat us," Molly said. "He only eats marshmallows. And tacos. Because everybody loves tacos. Even mysterious wild creatures who live in . . . **WAIT!**"

Molly skidded to a stop.

Kayley bumped into her.

"What is it?" Kayley whispered. "Is it **Littlefoot?**"

Molly pointed to some strange tracks. The tracks crossed the road and went along a small path through the bushes. They looked like huge footprints.

"It's definitely not Littlefoot," Molly said. "It must be **Bigfoot!** Dad wasn't making him up! Come on!"

Molly held up her camera and tip-toed along the short path. Kayley crept along behind her.

Through the bushes, they could see a small building. The footprints led right up to a door on the side of the building.

"It's Bigfoot's house!" Molly whispered.

"I don't think so," Kayley said. She pointed to a sign on the side of the building that said "Showers & Bathrooms."

"Do you think Bigfoot is taking a shower?" Kayley asked.

"Maybe," Molly said. "Or he might be—"

SCREEEECH!

The door of the building was pushed open by a big, hairy arm.

"It's Bigfoot!" cried Kayley. **"HIDE!"**

Kayley and Molly hopped into the bushes at the side of the path.

Molly held up her camera and took a picture just as the hairy creature stepped out of the building.

CLICK!

It started walking right toward them. It was wearing purple flip-flops and was holding a small basket full of shampoo, soap, and toothpaste.

It wasn't Bigfoot.

It was a hairy, smiling man.

"Good morning, ladies!" he said to Molly and Kayley as he passed by their hiding spot in the bushes.

He whistled a happy tune as he walked away down the path.

"That wasn't Bigfoot," Molly sighed.

"He was pretty hairy, though," Kayley said.

"Even hairier than Uncle Dave," Molly agreed. "But I still need to take an exciting picture."

"I know!" Kayley said. "You can take a picture of me doing a cannonball into the river! Let's go swimming!"

Chapter 6

Midnight Marshmallow Madness

Crackle, crackle, POP!

That night, they all sat around the campfire. Sparks danced through the air when Dad added another log to the roaring fire.

"I have a big surprise for tonight!" Dad sang.

"We're cooking tacos on sticks?" Molly asked.

"This is even better than tacos," Dad said.

"Excuse me, sir," Molly said. She patted Dad's arm. "I think we can all agree that nothing is better than tacos."

"Oh, this is," Dad said. He reached into a bag next to his chair.

"Did you get hippo spray?" asked Molly.

Dad shook his head. "I bought some more marshmallows at the camp store this afternoon while you were swimming with Mom."

"Hmmm . . . ," Molly said. "Marshmallows are just what I need tonight."

"Me, too," Dad said. "Marshmallows are just what I need every night!"

He popped one in his mouth.

"You ate it **raw?**" Molly gasped. "Can you do that?"

"I can," Dad said. "But you have to eat dinner first."

After dinner, everyone toasted marshmallows.

"Watch this!" Dad said.

He stuffed one marshmallow after another on his stick. Just as he was squeezing the tenth marshmallow on, his stick broke.

SNAP!

"Darn!" Dad said. "Now I need a new stick."

Mom turned on her flashlight. "I'll help you look," she said.

"Try to find a nice, strong one that can hold **FIFTY** marshmallows at once," Dad said.

"I'll try," laughed Mom.

They got up and looked around the campsite for a new stick for Dad.

Molly put her stick down and snuck over to the bag of marshmallows. She grabbed a handful of them.

"What are you doing with all those marshmallows, Molly?" asked Kayley.

Molly held a hand up to her lips. "Shhhhhh!" she whispered. "Don't ask."

"I'm asking," Kayley said.

Molly stuffed the marshmallows in her pocket. "Tonight, I'm going to sneak out of the tent and put these marshmallows on the ground. Then, when Littlefoot comes to eat them, I can take his picture!"

Molly sat back down just as Mom and Dad came back with a new stick.

"Oh, boy!" said Dad. **"Look at this beauty!"**

He held up a stick with four points on the end. "Can somebody hand me four marshmallows, please?"

When they were done toasting marshmallows, Dad packed up the food. He put the marshmallows safely in the cooler and latched it shut.

"We don't want any more midnight visitors," he said.

"Oh, yes we do," Molly chuckled.

Chapter 7

Midnight Visitor

Schhlllp. Schhhlllp. Schloop.

"Molly, what are you doing?" Kayley whispered.

"I'm trying to get these marshmallows out of my pocket," Molly whispered back. "I think they melted when I sat next to the fire."

She pulled her hand out of her pocket and licked the gooey mess off her fingers.

"I guess you won't be able to put them outside for Littlefoot," Kayley said.

"Maybe I can just lay my hand outside and wait for Littlefoot to come lick it," Molly said. She wiggled her sticky fingers in the air.

"Ewwww," groaned Kayley. "I don't think you should—"

"Shhhh!" Molly hissed. "Did you hear that?"

There was a small shuffling sound outside the tent.

Kayley's eyes grew wide. **"What is that?"** she whispered.

Molly picked up her camera. "It must be Littlefoot!" she whispered.

The shuffling sounds outside the tent stopped. There was a quiet squeak.

"He's opening the cooler to get the rest of the marshmallows!" Molly whispered.

Molly zipped open the tent flap and hopped out of the tent.

Something big was standing in front of the cooler stuffing marshmallows in its mouth.

"AH HA!" she cried. **"It's not Littlefoot. It's BIGFOOT!"**

She held up her camera.

Click!

The next day after breakfast, Molly and Kayley helped Mom and Dad pack up the campsite.

"Ohhhhh," Dad groaned. "I have such a stomachache."

"I'm not surprised," Mom said. "You ate almost the whole bag of marshmallows on your little midnight adventure last night."

"And I never got a picture of Littlefoot," Molly grumbled. "All I got was a picture of Dad with a face full of marshmallows. Maybe we can come back to the campground next weekend so I can have another try."

Dad groaned again. "I don't think we'll be camping for a while," he said.

"Maybe next weekend, we can go on a trip to the beach," Mom suggested.

"The beach?" Molly asked. She held up her camera and smiled. "Do we have any sea-monster spray?" she asked.

"Do I even want to know why you think you need sea-monster spray?" Mom asked.

"Probably not," Molly said.

All About Me!

A picture of me!

Name:
Marty Kelley

People in my family:
My lovely wife, Kerri
My amazing son, Alex
My terrific daughter, Tori

I really like: Pizza! And hiking in the woods. And being with my friends. And reading. And making music. And traveling with my family.

When I grow up I want to be:
A rock star drummer!

My special memory:
Sitting on the couch with my kids and reading a huge pile of books together.

Find more at my website: www.martykelley.com

≈ MORE ≈

MOLLY MAC

Meet Molly Mac, the curious
girl who is always onto
something. She's a whirlwind
full of questions, and she's
out to find the answers!

MOLLY MAC

≥ Lucky Break ≤
by MARTY KELLEY

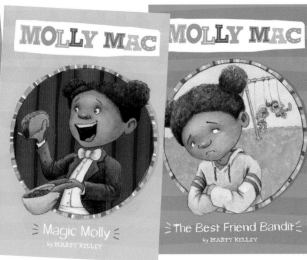

MOLLY MAC

≥ Magic Molly ≤
by MARTY KELLEY

MOLLY MAC

≥ The Best Friend Bandit ≤
by MARTY KELLEY

MOLLY MAC

≥ Sammy's Great Escape ≤
by MARTY KELLEY

MOLLY MAC

≥ Three...Two...One...Blastoff! ≤
by MARTY KELLEY

MOLLY MAC

≥ Top Secret Author Visit ≤
by MARTY KELLEY

THE FUN DOESN'T STOP HERE!

Discover more at
www.capstonekids.com

★ Videos & Contests
★ Games & Puzzles
★ Friends & Favorites
☆ Authors & Illustrators